For my grandparents, with love — S. N.

For Hugo, with love — G. A.

PUFFIN BOOKS

UK | USA | Canada | Ireland | Australia
India | New Zealand | South Africa

Puffin Books is part of the Penguin Random House group of companies
whose addresses can be found at global.penguinrandomhouse.com.

www.penguin.co.uk   www.puffin.co.uk   www.ladybird.co.uk

Penguin
Random House
UK

First published 2018

001

Text copyright © Giles Andreae, 2018
Illustrations copyright © Sandra Navarro / Lalalimola, 2018

The moral right of the author and illustrator has been asserted

Printed in China

A CIP catalogue record for this book is available from the British Library

ISBN: 978–0–141–37895–4

All correspondence to:
Puffin Books, Penguin Random House Children's
80 Strand, London WC2R 0RL

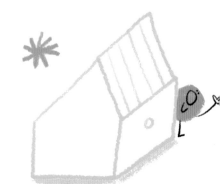

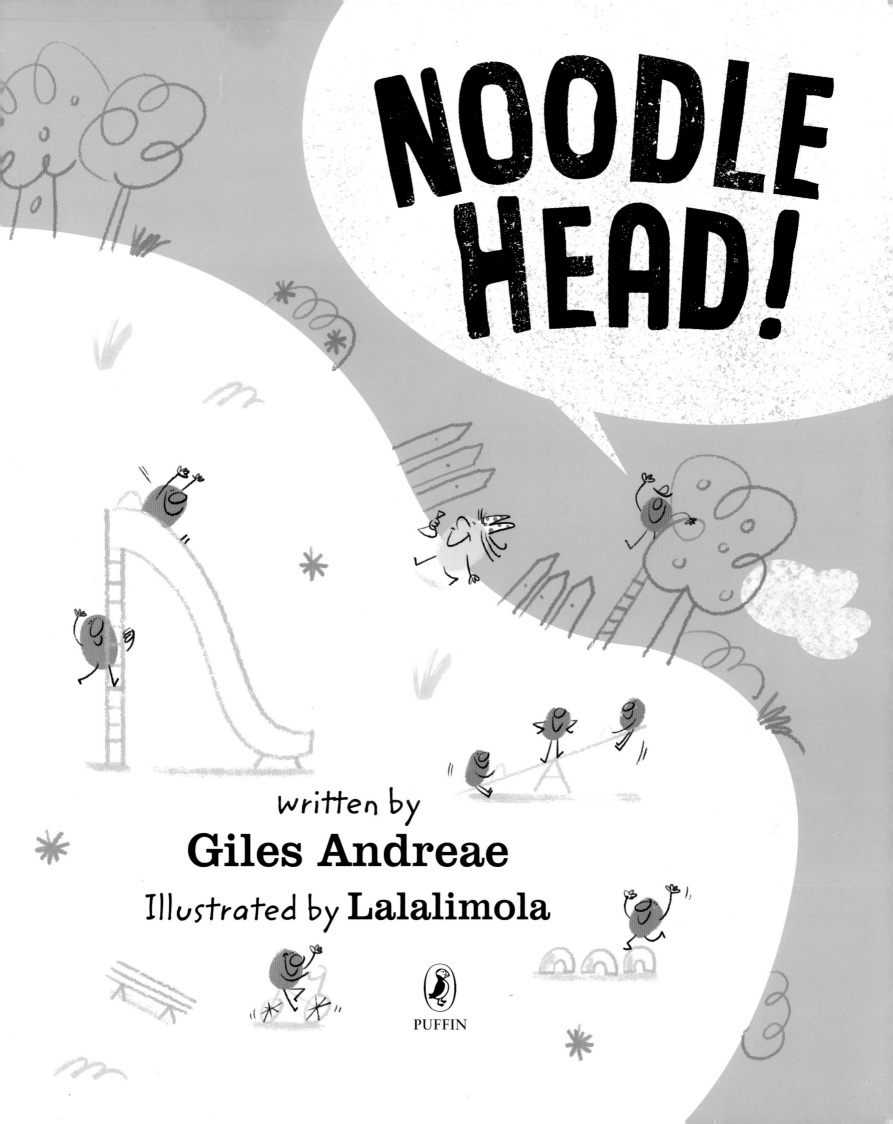

NOODLE HEAD!

written by
Giles Andreae

Illustrated by **Lalalimola**

PUFFIN

"**No,**" said Floppy.

"**Please?**"
said Flippy.

"**No,**" said Floppy again.

"**Silly socks!**" said Floppy.

"Bogey brain!"
said Flippy.

"Smelly sausage!" said Floppy.

"Potty pants!"
said Flippy.

"NOODLE

HEAD!"

they both yelled together.

"**Hmmm**, this isn't very nice," thought Floppy.

And she gave Flippy a sweet.

Flippy smiled.

"Rainbow face,"

he said.

"**Sunshine ears,**" said Floppy.

"**Twinkle bum**," *said Floppy.*

And, together, they **sat** . . .

and they **laughed** . . .

they **ate.**